D0298040

GROLIER
BOOK CLUB EDITION

Walt Disney's

BRER RABBIT
and his friends

From the motion picture *Song of the South*

Adapted from the original stories by Joel Chandler Harris

Copyright © 1973 by Walt Disney Productions. All rights reserved under Inter-
national and Pan-American Copyright Conventions. Published in the United States
by Random House, Inc., New York, and simultaneously in Canada by Random House
of Canada Limited, Toronto.

Library of Congress Cataloging in Publication Data
Main entry under title:
Walt Disney's Brer Rabbit and his friends.
(Disney's wonderful world of reading, no. 13)
Brer Rabbit outwits Brer Fox and Brer Bear when they try to trick him.
[1. Animals—Fiction. 2. Folklore, Negro] I. Title: Brer Rabbit and his friends.
PZ7.W16898   [398.2]   [E]   73-15623   ISBN 0-394-82774-0
ISBN 0-394-92774-5 (lib. bdg.)
Manufactured in the United States of America
           G H I J K
      6 7 8 9

Brer Rabbit lived in a brier patch.
It was full of twigs and stickers.
Nobody would ever want to go there.
But Brer Rabbit was small.
When he crawled in between those twigs,
he felt just as cozy as could be.

Brer Fox lived in a house.

It was full of chairs and pillows.

There was even a rug on the floor.

You might think that Brer Fox was happy.

But Brer Fox was not happy.

He knew that Brer Rabbit liked to play tricks on him.

But he never knew what the next trick would be.

One day Brer Fox planted some peanuts.
Brer Rabbit sat down to watch.

Brer Rabbit was surprised.

"Does that fox think he can keep me out of his peanut patch?" he said.

By and by the peanuts were ripe.
That night Brer Rabbit dug a hole
under the fence.

He filled his bag with peanuts and left.

And Brer Rabbit was glad to help
Brer Bear take his place in the air.

"If you see any crows," said Brer Rabbit,
"just make a scary face."

"Like this?" asked Brer Bear.

"That is a scary face," said Brer Rabbit.

"Thanks," said Brer Bear.

Brer Fox got some boards
and some nails.

He built a fence all the way around
his peanut patch.

Just then Brer Fox came to see
if Brer Rabbit was in the trap.
There was Brer Bear
hanging in the air
and making strange faces.

In the morning Brer Fox came
to see how his peanuts were doing.

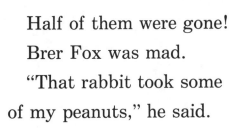

Half of them were gone!
Brer Fox was mad.
"That rabbit took some
of my peanuts," he said.

"Now how did he get in?"

Brer Fox looked all around.
At last he saw a little hole
under the fence.
"So this is how he got in,"
said Brer Fox.
"This gives me an idea."

Brer Fox got some rope and some stakes.

"That was Brer Rabbit's last trick," he said.

He made a trap next
to the little hole.

It was a trap to catch
Brer Rabbit.

That night Brer Rabbit
came back for the rest
of the peanuts.

When he crawled through the hole,
he stepped into the trap.
The rope grabbed him

and zipped him into the air.

You might think that
Brer Rabbit was scared.

But Brer Rabbit was not
scared.

"Does that fox think
I can't get out of this?"
said Brer Rabbit.

Early the next morning
Brer Bear came down the road.

"Howdy!" called Brer Rabbit.

"Howdy!" said Brer Bear.

"What are you doing up there?"

"Working," said Brer Rabbit.

"Working?" said Brer Bear.

"What kind of work is that?"

"Scarecrow work," said Brer Rabbit.

"Brer Fox pays a dollar a minute."

"Wow!" said Brer Bear.

"I wish I knew how to do scarecrow work."

"It is easy," said Brer Rabbit.

"Pull me down and I will show you how."

Brer Bear was glad to pull
Brer Rabbit down.

As soon as Brer Fox
saw Brer Rabbit,
he smelled trouble.

"When these peanuts
are ripe," said Brer Fox,
"that rabbit is going
to take them."

"So you are the peanut thief,"
cried Brer Fox.

"Peanut thief?" said Brer Bear.
"I'm no peanut thief. I'm your new scarecrow.
I took Brer Rabbit's place."

Brer Fox cut the rope and Brer Bear fell down.

"You are one dumb bear," said Brer Fox.

"That rabbit played a trick on you."

"Now listen here," said Brer Bear.
"I am not as dumb as you think.
You owe me a dollar.
Brer Rabbit said so."

"I don't owe you anything,"
said Brer Fox. "Can't you see
Brer Rabbit played a trick on us?"

"Then why don't we play a trick
on Brer Rabbit?" asked Brer Bear.
"You are not as dumb as I thought,"
said Brer Fox.

Brer Fox and Brer Bear got some stuffing
and some very sticky glue.

"Brer Rabbit is sure going to be surprised,"
said Brer Bear.

"That is not all he is going to be," said Brer Fox.

They made a stuffed rabbit.
They painted it with the very
sticky glue.

Then they took the stuffed rabbit
down the road to the brier patch.

Brer Fox and Brer Bear hid in the bushes.

Brer Rabbit came by and saw the stuffed rabbit.

"Howdy!" said Brer Rabbit.

But the stuffed rabbit did not say howdy.

"Can't you talk?" asked Brer Rabbit.

"Where are your manners?"

The stuffed rabbit just sat there.

Brer Rabbit was mad.

"If you don't say howdy
by the time I count to three,
I am going to punch you in the nose.
One,
   two,
      three!"

Brer Rabbit punched him in the nose.

His hand stuck in that sticky glue.

"Let me go," cried Brer Rabbit,

"or I will punch you again."

The stuffed rabbit did not let go.

Brer Rabbit punched him again.

Now both hands were stuck in the glue.

Brer Rabbit was REALLY mad.

"Take this!" cried Brer Rabbit.

He kicked him
with his right foot.

"And this!" cried Brer Rabbit.
He kicked him with his left foot.

Now Brer Rabbit was as stuck as he could be.

His hands were stuck.

His feet were stuck.

Even his ears were stuck.

Brer Fox and Brer Bear jumped out of the bushes.

"Your tricks are over, Brer Rabbit,"
said Brer Fox.
"As soon as we fix a fire,
we are going to roast you.
I can hardly wait!"

"Is THAT all?" said Brer Rabbit.
"I was afraid you were going
to throw me in the brier patch."

"I don't think Brer Rabbit is scared
of roasting," said Brer Bear.

"Then we won't roast him," said Brer Fox.
"We will hang him."

"I don't care what you do," said Brer Rabbit.
"Just don't throw me in the brier patch."

"I don't think Brer Rabbit is scared
of hanging," said Brer Bear.

"Then we won't hang him," said Brer Fox.
"We will drown him."

"Roast me, hang me, drown me," said
Brer Rabbit. "But please, *please*, PLEASE—
don't throw me in the brier patch!"

"I don't think Brer Rabbit
is scared of drowning,"
said Brer Bear.
"But he sure is scared
of that brier patch."

Just then Brer Fox had an idea.
"I know!" said Brer Fox.
"We will throw him in the brier patch."

So Brer Bear
yanked Brer Rabbit
out of the glue
and threw him—
KERBLAM—
right into
the middle
of the brier patch.

Brer Fox and Brer Bear
started dancing.

"That rabbit is GONE FOREVER,"
cried Brer Fox.

Just then they heard a voice.
It was coming from the brier patch.

It was Brer Rabbit!

"Me—gone forever?" called Brer Rabbit.

"I'm not gone. I'm HOME.

I told you not to throw me

in the brier patch.

The brier patch is where I live."

"This was your dumb idea," said Brer Fox.

"No, it was your dumb idea," said Brer Bear.

But Brer Rabbit did not
wait around to see who was right.

He was off to get the rest
of the peanuts.